NEW

Block Busters

WA

D0492513

WALTHAM FOREST	
027243322	
PETERS	16-Mar-07
£4.99	JF

Block Busters

Robin and Chris Lawrie

Illustrated by
Robin Lawrie

Acknowledgements

The authors and publishers would like to thank
Julia Francis, Hereford Diocesan Deaf Church
lay co-chaplain, for her help with the sign language
in the *Chain Gang* books.

Published by Evans Brothers Limited
2A Portman Mansions
Chiltern Street
London W1U 6NR

© Robin and Christine Lawrie

First published 2001

The authors assert their moral right to be identified as the
authors of this work in accordance with the Copyright, Designs
and Patents Act, 1988.

Printed in Hong Kong

All rights reserved. No part of this publication may be
reproduced, stored in a retrieval system or transmitted,
in any form or by any means, electronic, mechanical,
photocopying, recording or otherwise, without prior
permission of Evans Brothers Limited.

British Library Cataloguing in Publication data.
Lawrie, Robin
  Block Busters. – (The Chain Gang)
  1. Slam Duncan (Fictitious character) – Juvenile fiction
  2. All terrain cycling – Juvenile fiction 3. Adventure stories
  4. Children's stories
  I. Title II. Lawrie, Chris
  823.9'14[J]

ISBN 0 237 52263 2

Hi, my name is "Slam" Duncan. I ride and race downhill mountain bikes with a group of friends called "The Chain Gang".

I'm Aziz- call me 'Dozy.' I'm Fionn. I'm Larry.

We are doing a race series called the "Sword in the Stump Challenge". It's for duel descender and cross-country riders as well as downhillers. The idea is to promote sportsmanship and fair play by making us think about King Arthur and his Knights of the Round Table. We are halfway through the series and the next race is the second cross-country event.

* I'm Andy. (Andy is deaf and signs instead of talking.)

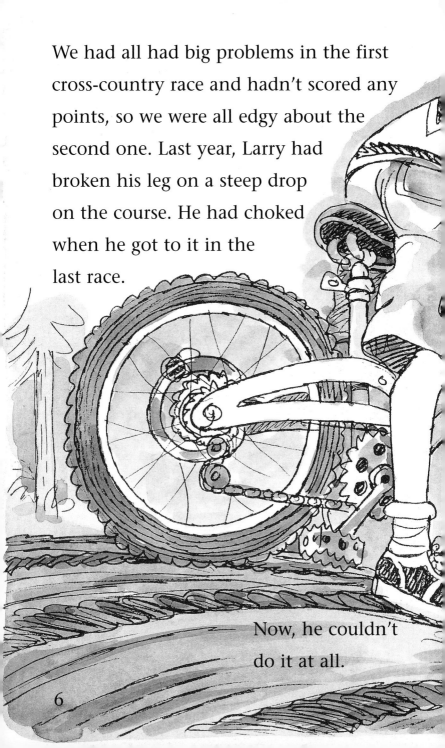

We had all had big problems in the first cross-country race and hadn't scored any points, so we were all edgy about the second one. Last year, Larry had broken his leg on a steep drop on the course. He had choked when he got to it in the last race.

Now, he couldn't do it at all.

6

7

Some spectators had been rude to Fionn in the last race. It had sapped her confidence.

Now she was making mistakes.

Dozy had been on the wrong tyres
and he had made a mess of things.

He was determined
not to make the
same mistake
again. So he
loaded all kinds
of information
about tyres
on to his
computer.

9

Andy had a different problem.

He'd had a bad crash during the last cross-country race.

He had been unable to hear a rider trying to get past him. So the rider had pushed him off the track. Andy was afraid it would happen again.

Serves you right, CREEP!

11

I never really got going during the last race. Now I was practising hard, but I was crashing a lot. I thought it was because my reactions were getting slow. I decided a good computer game might sharpen me up.

So I scraped the mud off my bike and paid a visit to Steady Eddy's stall in the market.

I bought "Space Bikers". It was very cheap and looked like fun.

I couldn't wait to play it, but when I tried to install it . . .

I knew Dozy's computer had lots of
memory, so I went round to his place.
He'd gone out
for a minute,
but his mum let me into his room.

His computer was on.
There was a lot of
stuff about tyres on it.
It looked boring, so
I pressed a few buttons
and made it disappear.

14

I loaded "Space Bikers" and
waited a few minutes . . .

The computer froze. I should never have
bought a video game from Steady Eddy.
Then Dozy walked in. I thought he was
going to hit me. But instead he called a

gang meeting
for the next
day at the
round table
in the school library.

Next day:

King Arthur would have asked Merlin to use magic if his knights were losing battles. For us, **SPORTS PSYCHOLOGY** is the answer. We've all got **MENTAL BLOCKS.** So I'm going to give you all **BLOCK BUSTERS.** But first you have to tell me what your blocks are. Mine is tyres.

Andy signed:

1. Can't 2. hear 3. riders 4. overtaking. 5. I'm a 6. danger.

LOYALTY   FAIR PLAY

SHARING

16

LOYALTY
FAIR PLAY
I can't handle the insults any more. My confidence is gone.
I just can't face that big drop where I broke my leg.
Tales of Chivalry
KNIGHTS of the ROUND TABLE
I just feel negative about everything. Can't go fast enough, can't overtake, can't jump, can't climb...
O K. I'll deal with you all tomorrow, starting with you, Slam.
SHARING

18

19

OK, Larry, what's your problem?

NERVES, Dozy, it's my NERVES. I'm fine on the course until I get to that drop where I broke my leg, then I just go to pieces. People have started calling it "Break-a-Leg Drop". It's not funny.

Dozy scribbled something on a piece of paper and put it in an envelope.

Here. Your very own block buster. Open it when you get to Break-a-Leg drop.

Who's next?

Larry

21

Andy came in. Dozy gave him
two rear-view mirrors.
No-one could sneak up
on him with those!

Fionn was next. Dozy knew that Fionn
loves shopping. He put her in front of
the computer. The screen filled with
"DOZY'S VICTORY SHOP".

OK, Fionn, choose
what you need.

Welcome TO DOZY'S VICTORY SHOP
EVERYTHING YOU NEED TO WIN

SHOPPING BASKET

ITEMS IN BASKET
O
GO TO CHECKOUT.

COURAGE   ORDER □
STAMINA   ORDER □
CONFIDENCE   ORDER □
STRENGTH   ORDER. □
STYLE   ORDER □
SPEED   ORDER □

Fionn clicked the "Order" buttons on the items she wanted. Then she clicked "Go to checkout".

Dozy gave Fionn a little bike basket for her handlebars. It had four packets in it, and a little lid to stop them falling out.

9:00 a.m. on race day. Everyone was at the start line.

24

Lads start first, from the front. Girls line up at the back. Two six-mile laps were ahead of us.

Fionn's VICTORY basket.

Woooo Woooo... LOVE the basket, Fionn!

Hey, Larry, love the SHORTS!

Hey, Fionn, what's the basket for? Your DOLLIES?

Mine got ripped. These are my dad's.

Larry's BLOCKBUSTER envelope.

BANG!

We were off!

25

I was doing well
up the start-line climb.
At the top, the course
dropped away, with a big
jump at the bottom.

I CAN'T!

Then I remembered
the bell.

RING
RING!

Suddenly
I felt much better.

RING RING!

It was nothing short of magic. Dozy's "Replace" tool had worked.

OOOOOHHHH!!!

It was one of my best jumps ever.

Five minutes later, I looked behind me. Fionn was right there.

She went straight past me. Nobody was making fun of her any more.

Then I came up behind Larry.

He had frozen at the edge of "Break-a-leg Drop".

I saw him open his block buster envelope and start laughing fit to bust. Still laughing, he pulled up his baggy shorts, stood on the pedals, got his weight over the back wheel and rode the drop-off like a pro.

I followed him down.

So, what was in the note?

It said: "Imagine the worst thing that could happen right now." And I imagined...

Somehow the drop-off didn't seem so bad.

29

At the bottom of the last climb, we saw
Dozy grinding his way up
through the mud. His
carefully chosen tyres
were really working
well for him.
He was just
behind Andy
who was trying
to catch
the main
pack of riders.

We went up after them but there was
no way we were ever going
to catch them.

We saw Dozy try to
overtake Andy on the left.

Andy saw him in his mirror
and blocked him.

Then Dozy tried to pass on the right.
Andy saw that, too, and put on
a burst of speed,
leaving Dozy
way behind.

We got to
the top
just in time to see
Andy roaring past
the pack on the last
descent to the finish line.
Going downhill, he was ace!

It was close, but Andy came in first and Fionn, not far behind, won the girls' race.

While they were collecting their prizes, Larry and I thanked Dozy for his help. In spite of being downhillers, we had all scored some points for the Sword in the Stump Challenge.

Later that night, Dozy and I were checking his e-mails. There was one from Andy:

Mirror, mirror, left and right,
Keeping Dozy well in sight.
Thanks to him I won the race
But as a chum, HE's in first place.
ANDY